Ladybird  Readers

Decepticons in the Scrapyard

Series Editor: Sorrel Pitts
Adapted by Hazel Geatches

LADYBIRD BOOKS

UK | USA | Canada | Ireland | Australia
India | New Zealand | South Africa

Ladybird Books is part of the Penguin Random House group of companies
whose addresses can be found at global.penguinrandomhouse.com.
www.penguin.co.uk   www.puffin.co.uk   www.ladybird.co.uk

First published 2018
001

Licensed by:

Printed in China

A CIP catalogue record for this book is available from the British Library

ISBN: 978-0-241-31943-7

All correspondence to
Ladybird Books
Penguin Random House Children's
80 Strand, London WC2R 0RL

MIX
Paper from
responsible sources
FSC® C018179

Ladybird Readers

Decepticons in the Scrapyard

Picture words

Denny

Russell

Steeljaw
(a Decepticon)

Autobots

Fixit

Bumblebee

Strongarm

Grimlock

Sideswipe

forest

scrapyard

computer

gate

scanner

Decepticons

fight (verb)

drive (verb)

Russell and Denny
are in the scrapyard.

"The Autobots like living with us," says Russell.

"Yes," says Denny, "and they like helping people."

Fixit is watching his scanner.

"I can see Decepticons in the forest," he says. "Bumblebee, go and find them!"

"Let's go!" Bumblebee says
to the Autobots.

"Oh no! Now the gate is open!" says Fixit.

Russell, Denny, and Fixit run to the gate.

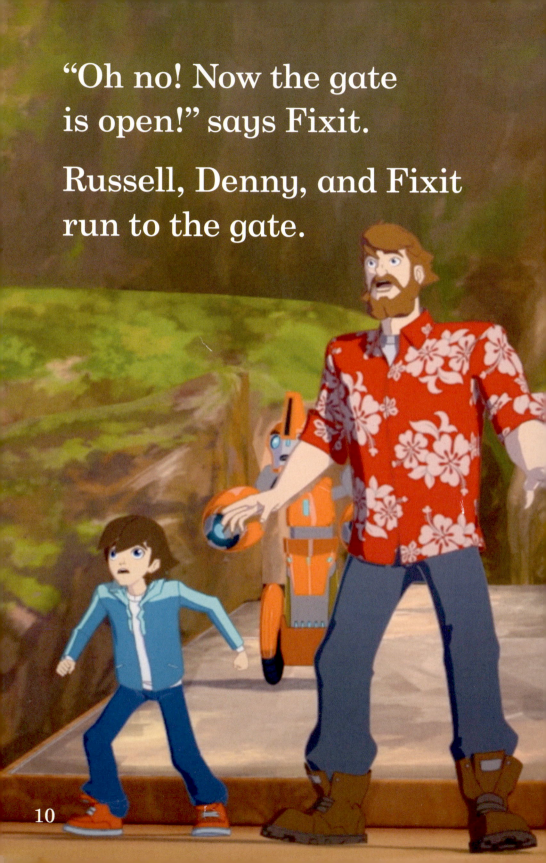

They see Steeljaw and
his Decepticon friends
in the scrapyard!

The Decepticons have big arms, and they catch Russell and Denny.

"Ow!" says Russell.

Then, a Decepticon goes to Fixit's computer. "This is our computer now!" he says.

The Autobots come back from the forest.

They see the Decepticons.

"Where are Russell and
Denny?" asks Bumblebee.

"They are here!"
says Steeljaw.

"I want this scrapyard!"
he says.

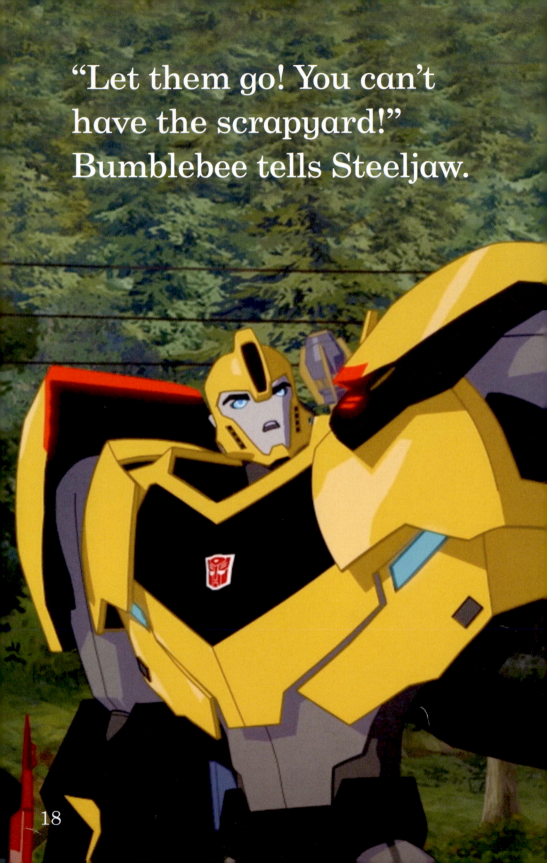

"Let them go! You can't have the scrapyard!" Bumblebee tells Steeljaw.

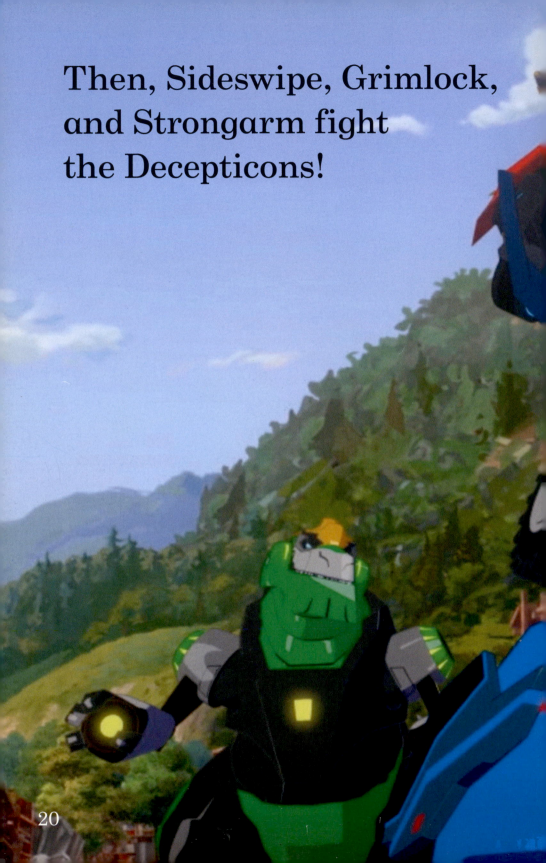

Then, Sideswipe, Grimlock, and Strongarm fight the Decepticons!

"You can't have the scrapyard! Now go!" says Bumblebee.

Steeljaw and the Decepticons drive from the scrapyard.

Then, Russell and Denny run to the computer.

"The computer is closing the gate," says Denny. "The Decepticons can't come back."

"Thank you, Russell and Denny. People are great!" says Bumblebee.

"Autobots are great, too!"
says Denny. "Now we have
our scrapyard again."

Activities

The key below describes the skills practiced in each activity.

Spelling and writing

Reading

Speaking

? Critical thinking

Preparation for the Cambridge Young Learners exams

Look at the letters.
Write the words. ✏️ ⬢

1 D n y e n

D e n n y

2 l s e R l u s

....

3 e B b l u m

.... b e e

4 m r a

S t r o n g ....

5 F i i t x

....

29

2 **Look and read. Write *yes* or *no*.**

Russell and Denny are in the scrapyard.

"The Autobots like living with us," says Russell.

"Yes," says Denny, "and they like helping people."

1 Russell and Denny are people. <u>yes</u>

2 Denny is an Autobot. ....

3 Russell and Denny are in the forest. ....

4 Autobots like living with people. ....

3 **Look and read. Put a ✓ or a ✗ in the boxes.** 📖 ❇️

1   This is a scrapyard.   ✓

2   This is a forest.   ☐

3   This is a computer.   ☐

4   This is a window.   ☐

5   They are fighting.   ☐

4 **Circle the correct words.**

Fixit is watching his scanner.

"I can see Decepticons in the forest," he says. "Bumblebee, go and find them!"

"Let's go!" Bumblebee says to the Autobots.

8

9

1 **Bumblebee /** **Fixit**
is watching his scanner.

2 "I can see **Autobots,"** /
Decepticons," says Fixit.

3 "They are in the
forest," / **scrapyard,"**
says Fixit.

4 "Bumblebee, go and find
them!" / **us!"** says Fixit.

5 **Circle the correct sentences.**

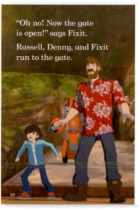
"Oh no! Now the gate is open!" says Fixit.

Russell, Denny, and Fixit run to the gate.

They see Steeljaw and his Decepticon friends in the scrapyard!

1 **a** "Oh no!" says Fixit.
    b "Oh no!" says Denny.

2 **a** Russell, Denny, and Fixit walk to the gate.
    b Russell, Denny, and Fixit run to the gate.

3 **a** They see Bumblebee and his friends.
    b They see Steeljaw and his Decepticon friends.

4 **a** Steeljaw is in the scrapyard.
    b Steeljaw is in the forest.

6 **Find the words.**

fight m g a t o r e s t s c e g a t e c a n s c a n n e r e s t s c r a p y a r d p l y

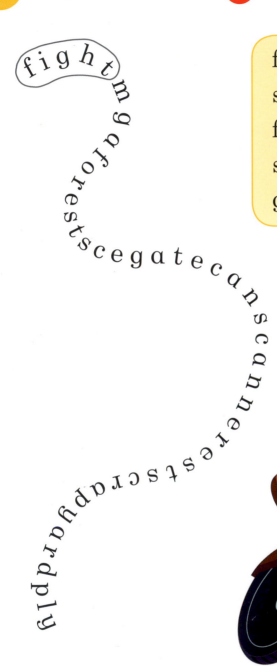

fight
scanner
forest
scrapyard
gate

7 Talk with a friend about the pictures. One picture is different. How is it different? 🔴 ❓

1

Picture c is different, because Fixit is not a person.

8 Look at the picture and read the questions. Write the answers.

1 Who do the Decepticons catch?
The Decepticons catch
Russell and Denny .

2 How do they catch them?
They catch them in their

.

3 Who goes to Fixit's computer?
A

goes to Fixit's computer.

9 **Look and read. Choose the correct words, and write them on the lines.**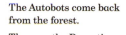

The Autobots come back from the forest.

They see the Decepticons.

"Where are Russell and Denny?" asks Bumblebee.

---

gate   Bumblebee   Decepticons   forest

1 The scrapyard ⎯⎯ gate ⎯⎯ is open.

2 The Autobots come back from the ⎯⎯⎯⎯⎯⎯⎯.

3 They see the ⎯⎯⎯⎯⎯⎯⎯.

4 "Where are Russell and Denny?" asks ⎯⎯⎯⎯⎯⎯⎯.

10 **Circle the correct pictures.**

1 Where do the Autobots live?

2 Who fights the Autobots?

3 Who catches Russell and Denny?

4 What does Steeljaw want?

11 **Talk to a friend about Autobots and Decepticons.** 💬 ❓

1

> Who are the Autobots' friends?

> Denny and Russell are their friends.

2 Why are they friends, do you think?

3 Why does Steeljaw want the scrapyard, do you think?

12 Who says this?

Fixit   Bumblebee   Russell   Steeljaw

1 "Oh no! Now the gate is open!" says ___Fixit___ .

2 "Ow!" says

_____ .

3 "Where are Russell and Denny?" asks _____ .

4 "They are here!" says

_____ .

5 "Thank you, Russell and Denny!" says _____ .

13 **Find the words.**

d	e	c	e	f	o	r	e	s	t	b
s	c	r	a	p	y	a	r	d	a	t
b	o	m	n	w	o	r	i	w	b	s
w	m	t	l	a	m	x	m	z	p	c
l	p	v	f	s	p	i	m	e	o	a
b	u	p	i	d	u	n	i	i	n	n
s	t	b	g	e	t	h	a	w	i	n
g	e	d	h	q	e	i	p	e	a	e
i	r	d	t	n	r	g	a	t	e	r

forest

computer

scrapyard

gate

fight

scanner

14 **Read the questions.**
Write the answers. 📖 ✏️

Then, Sideswipe, Grimlock, and Strongarm fight the Decepticons!

1 Who wants the scrapyard?

Steeljaw

2 Who catches Denny and Russell?

3 Who fights the Decepticons?

4 Where do they fight?

15 **Circle the correct words.**

1 Who says to Steeljaw, "You can't have the scrapyard! Now go!"

   a Russell   **b** Bumblebee

2 Who do the Autobots fight?

   a Denny   **b** the Decepticons

3 Where do Russell and Denny run to?

   a the forest   **b** the computer

4 What is the computer closing?

   a the gate   **b** the scanner

16 **Order the story. Write 1—4.**

.... Steeljaw and the Decepticons
drive from the scrapyard.

.... Sideswipe, Grimlock, and
Strongarm fight the Decepticons!

___1___ Fixit is watching his scanner. He
can see Decepticons in the forest.

.... The Decepticons catch Russell
and Denny.

17 Put a by the Autobots.

1 Bumblebee

2 Grimlock

3 Steeljaw

4 Fixit

5 Russell

6 Denny

7 Sideswipe

8 Strongarm

18 Read the text. Choose the correct words and write them next to 1—4.

1	Decepticons	Autobots	Steeljaw
2	Decepticons	Russell	people
3	car	scanner	scrapyard
4	car	gate	computer

Russell and Denny are friends with the

¹ Autobots . Autobots like helping

² _____. The Decepticons are

in the ³ _____. They catch

Russell and Denny. Then, a Decepticon

goes to Fixit's ⁴ _____.

19 **Draw a picture of your favorite Autobot or Decepticon. Answer the questions.** 📖 ✏️

1 What is the name of your favorite Autobot or Decepticon?

Its name is ....

2 Is it good or bad?

It is ....

Level 1

Anansi Helps a Friend	Cinderella	The Enormous Turnip	On the Farm	Cars
978-0-241-25409-7	978-0-241-25407-3	978-0-241-25408-0	978-0-241-25413-4	978-0-241-28354-7
Jon's Football Team	The Magic Porridge Pot	In the Garden	Fun with Old Things	Fairy Friends
978-0-241-25411-0	978-0-241-25406-6	978-0-241-26220-7	978-0-241-26219-1	978-0-241-28351-6
Peter Rabbit Goes to the Island	Topsy and Tim Go to the Zoo	Topsy and Tim Go to the Farm	The Fair	Daddy Pig's Old Chair
978-0-241-25415-8	978-0-241-25414-1	978-0-241-28355-4	978-0-241-28357-8	978-0-241-28356-1
Rex the Big Dinosaur	Peter Rabbit and the Radish Robber	Topsy and Tim Go to London	On a Boat	Baby Animals
978-0-241-29741-4	978-0-241-29742-1	978-0-241-29743-8	978-0-241-29744-5	978-0-241-29745-2
The Tale of Peter Rabbit	Going Swimming	Decepticons in the Scrapyard	Deserts	
978-0-241-31614-6	978-0-241-31613-9	978-0-241-31943-7	978-0-241-31608-5	

Now you're ready for Level 2!